Frog's flicky licky tongue

This book belongs to...

....

Frog's flicky licky tongue

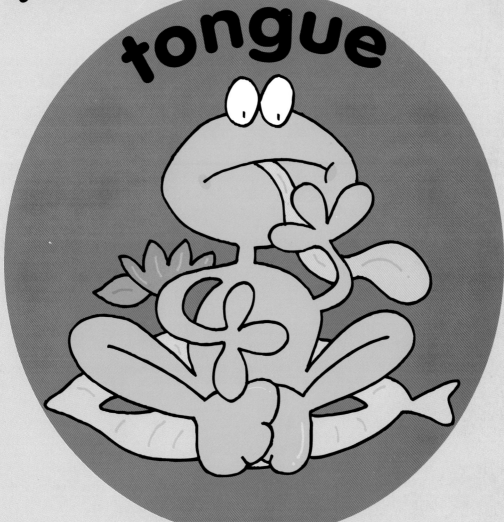

Written by Jillian Harker
Illustrated by Simon Abbott

Bright ☆ Sparks

Frog sat on a log beside the pond at Goosefeather Farm. He turned his head first one way and then the other. He was on the look-out for flies, because he was hungry! Suddenly, a large one flitted past. Frog flicked out his tongue – **SPLAT!**

It missed the fly and hit Duck on the back of her head!

"Please be more careful!" quacked Duck.

"Sorry!" said Frog and hopped off down the lane, after the fly.

It wasn't long before Frog saw the fly in the field, buzzing around Horse's head.

"Oooh!" said Frog, "yummy!"

He flicked out his tongue – **SPLAT!** – and missed! His tongue caught in Horse's mane!

"Hey, watch out!" neighed Horse.

"Sorry," mumbled Frog and he hopped into the farmyard, in search of the fly.

In the farmyard, Hen was busy pecking at her corn. Frog saw the fly buzzing around her.

"Oh, there you are," he said and flicked out his tongue – **SPLAT!**

But he missed again. His tongue wrapped around Hen's leg, tripping her up!

"Look where you're flicking that tongue of yours!" clucked Hen.

"Sorry," said Frog quietly and he hopped away—he *would* catch that pesky fly!

Cat was lying in a sunny corner of the farmyard. Nearby, the fly was buzzing around one of her kittens.

"At last!" said Frog. He quickly flicked out his tongue—**SPLAT!**

It shot past the fly and curled around the kitten's tail.

"Miaow!" wailed the kitten. "Help! Mummy! Help!"

"Shoo!" shouted Cat.

Frog jumped in fright and hopped off towards the pond – where was that juicy fly?

When he reached the pond, the fly was nowhere to be seen. So, Frog decided to hop onto a lily pad for a rest. He knew he had made the other animals very cross. Maybe he should keep out of their way for a while.

But his tummy rumbled and grumbled! Where was that fly?

At the farm, the animals were furious!

"I've got a headache," complained Duck.

"My mane is all tangled," moaned Horse.

"Well, my leg really hurts," grumbled Hen.

"And my kitten is still in shock!" wailed Cat.

"That frog needs to be taught how to catch flies properly," said Duck. "Who's going to show him?"

"ME!" they all yelled together.

So, Duck swam up to Frog.

"We've all decided you need lessons in catching food," she said. "Come on."

Frog followed Duck to the middle of the pond.

"Now look, it's simple," said Duck. "Open your mouth and scoop up the insects. There are plenty floating on top of the water."

Frog tried to copy Duck, but all he got was a
mouthful of water!
"Oh, Duck!" he glugged.
"I can't do what you do. I haven't got a big
beak to scoop with."

"Never mind,
Frog!" said Duck.
"Maybe Horse
can help you."

"Yes, Frog, hop over and *I'll* show you how to catch flies," called Horse. "There are plenty of midges here. Open your mouth with your teeth wide apart, then snap them shut."

So, Frog opened his mouth, just like Horse had shown him and tried to snap it shut. But, instead of a lovely meal of midges, he just got a mouthful of air!

"Oh, Horse!" he gulped.
"I can't do what you do. I haven't any teeth!"

"I know what the problem is," said Hen. "You aren't bobbing your head forward. Try doing it like I do."

And she pecked at the floor to show him.

Frog quickly jerked his head forward, just as Hen had done—and toppled over!

"Oh, Hen!" said Frog, sadly. "I can't do what you do. I haven't got a neck like yours."

"Don't just use your mouth, Frog," called
Cat. "You need to use your front legs, too.
Watch what I do." And she showed Frog how
to stretch out his legs and pounce on his prey.

Frog tried really hard to copy her,
but his front legs were just *too* short.

"It's no good, Cat,"

said Frog. "I'm never going to learn.
I'm just going to be hungry *for ever!*"

Suddenly, there was the sound of a loud bell – **DING! DONG!**

It was Cow!

"I hope you don't mind my saying so," she said, "but I don't think any of you are right for this job."

"And I suppose *you* are?" clucked Hen.

"Well," said Cow, "have any of you ever caught a fly?"

There was silence.

"Exactly!" said Cow.

"But *you* don't eat flies!" said Duck.

"No," giggled Cow. "But they bother me *all* the time. I have to be able to hit them out of the way with my tail. So I know *exactly* how to aim and get them."

"Oh, please tell me quickly," begged Frog.
"I'm so hungry."

"Well, Frog," said Cow, "flies move very fast. If you aim for where they are, they're gone by the time you get there. Aim for where they're going and you'll get them every time!"

So, Frog tried it. He sat on a leaf and waited. Before long, the big, fat fly he was chasing earlier came buzzing by. He watched where it was heading, took aim and... **SPLAT!** – one juicy fly for lunch!

Frog tried again and again. It worked every time and his tummy grew fatter and fatter.

"Thank you, Cow!" said Frog. "You're a very good teacher."

"I hope you are, too, Frog," laughed Cow, "because I'd *love* to learn to swim!"

Bright ★ Sparks

Thank you for buying this Bright Sparks book.

We donate one book to less fortunate children for every two sold.
We have already donated over 150,000 books.

We want to help the world to read.

This is a Bright Sparks book.
First published in 2002.
Bright Sparks,
Queen Street House, 4 Queen Street,
BATH BA1 1HE, UK
Copyright © Parragon 2002

Written by Jillian Harker
Illustrated by Simon Abbott

Printed in China.
ISBN 1-84250-534-3